KARATE

Fiona Parker

photographs by Mark Coote

CONTENTS

Page 2   History
Page 3   The Place
Page 4   The Moves
Page 6   Grading
Page 8   Respect

Learning Media

HISTORY

Karate came from Japan many years ago.
The word "karate" comes from two Japanese words:
"kara," which means "empty," and "te," which means "hand."
So, karate means "empty hand" in Japanese.
Today, people from many different countries learn karate.

THE PLACE

There are dojos all over the world.
A "dojo" is a place
where you learn karate.
You take off your shoes
before you go into a dojo.

THE MOVES

When you're training, you wear practice clothes called "gi." You do warm-up exercises, such as push-ups and stretches. Then you practice your moves. There are three main moves to practice, called kicking, blocking, and punching.

It can be noisy in the dojo.
That's because when you are
kicking, blocking, or punching,
you make a loud noise
at the same time.
This loud noise, or shout,
is called a "kiai."

GRADING

If you do karate, you work hard to get better. As you get better, you can take a test called a "grading." If you pass the test, you get a new colored belt to wear.

You start out with a white belt.
As you get better, you go to
blue, yellow, green,
and brown belts.
The last and highest grading
is for the black belt.

RESPECT

Karate these days is about keeping fit. Most of all, it is about confidence, self-control, and respect – that's respect for yourself and for other people.